The Barber's Christmas Bride

Mail Order Brides of Dayton Falls

(Book Two)

Copyright

Table of Contents

Dedication

To Margaret Tanner, my very dear friend and fellow author, for her enduring encouragement and friendship.

To Alan, my husband of over forty-eight years, who has been a relentless supporter of my writing and dreams for many years.

To You, my wonderful readers, who encourage me to continue writing these stories. It is such a joy knowing so many of you enjoy reading my stories as much as I love writing them for you.

Chapter One

Westlake, Wyoming – 1880

Allie MacIntosh reeled from the forceful slap that landed on her face.

She picked herself up from the floor and faced her attacker.

Her head was spinning, and her eyes stung with tears, but she would not show her pain. Nor would she put her hand to her cheek, even though she desperately wanted to.

Instead she apologized for something she didn't do. "I'm very sorry, Sir," she said, then turned and walked out of the room.

Mrs Montgomery minced after her. "It's your own fault, Allie," she said. "I've warned you time and again not to intimidate the Master." Her eyes glared at Allie, as though *she* was the problem.

"Yes, Ma'am," she said meekly. "Of course, you are right." This job was all she had. She might be a meagre servant, but at least it was a job.

She couldn't afford to lose it.

"You may go." Mrs Montgomery waved her hands through the air, then went on her merry way, leaving Allie staring after her.

She'd put up with years of verbal abuse from Mr Montgomery, but since Charlotte had left to become a mail order bride, he'd become physically abusive too. She no longer wanted to go to work, and she was fearful of her life.

What the Master would do if he found out she'd been corresponding with his daughter, she didn't know. All her mail came through Miss Bethany at the Mail Order Bride Agency – it wouldn't do for him to find it.

Miss Charlotte had even suggested she register for herself. For her own safety, but Allie had brushed her suggestion aside.

But no more.

She couldn't risk being killed at the hands of this mad tyrant.

On her next day off she would visit Miss Bethany.

* * *

Charlie Jones swept the hair off the floor of his barber shop.

It had been a slow day, but he was hopeful it would pick up. He glanced up expectantly when he heard the shop door open.

"Good morning, Charlie."

"Morning Sheriff," he said with a smile.

Angus Doyle pulled his hat from his head and fiddled with it.

"It's a while since I've seen you in here, Sheriff." He put the broom aside. "I was beginning to wonder if that new bride of yours was cutting your hair."

Angus laughed. "Charlotte has more than enough to do with our growing brood," he said. "No, it just came down to time. As you can see, it's been quite a while between cuts."

Charlie nodded. "Well sit yourself down then, Sheriff." He flicked his barber's cape and wrapped it around his customer's neck. "Cut and shave?"

Angus put a hand to his chin. "Both," he said, then settled in.

"How have you been, Charlie? I haven't seen much of you lately."

He wondered if Angus was genuinely interested, or just making small talk.

Charlie started to clip away at the sheriff's hair. "I keep myself busy," he said. "Between the shop and home, I ain't got much time for anything else."

Angus stared hard at him in the mirror. "You need a wife, Charlie."

Charlie's head shot up. "You're not serious, surely?"

Then he smiled. The sheriff must be having a joke with him. Very funny. Only…

"Where did you meet your missus?" he asked. "I never did hear." He continued to cut at Angus's hair but was more thoughtful about getting a bride.

Only trouble was, where to find her. There weren't many women in Dayton Falls. Ones that weren't married anyways.

"Between you and me? Mail order bride. Worked out perfectly for me." He looked up at Charlie's thoughtful expression. "Talk to Pete at the post office. He did it before me."

"Worthwhile?"

"Definitely worthwhile," Angus told him.

"I might just do that," Charlie said, rubbing his chin. "Now stop talkin' Sheriff, so I can give you a shave."

* * *

Allie hesitated as she stood in the doorway of the Westlake Mail Order Bride Agency.

Charlotte had told her about the perfect match she'd had with Angus Doyle, and how much in love they were. If only she could get a similar result.

She looked up toward the door at the top of the stairs. There was a small unobtrusive sign on the door.

It was very discreet, which was what she needed. She certainly didn't need the Montgomery's knowing what she was contemplating.

She pulled her bonnet further around her face, lifted her skirts, and trudged to the top of the stairs.

Taking a deep breath, Allie knocked on the door.

"Come in."

She stood for what seemed forever. *Was this really what she wanted?* Right now, she had a secure job, there was money coming in regularly, and she was able to help her parents out.

It didn't take long for Allie to conclude it was a matter of life and death. If she continued the way things were now, Mr Montgomery was likely to eventually knock her cold stone dead as his violence was escalating.

She lifted her skirts and scampered into the small room before she changed her mind.

The middle-aged woman seemed shocked to see her but smiled at her regardless. "Can I help you, Allie?"

They knew each other because of Charlotte's letters, but Miss Bethany Wilde had no idea of what was about to transpire.

"I, I," She didn't know why she was so hesitant. She needed to do this. "I want to be a mail order bride."

Miss Bethany's eyes opened wide. "Really? I thought you enjoyed your job." She sat down behind the big desk and motioned for Allie to sit opposite.

"I can't stay there anymore." She slowly turned her head to the side until the latest bruise was visible to the older woman.

She gasped. "Mr. Montgomery did this?" Her voice was almost a screech.

Allie nodded, then lifted her hand to her face. "I'm afraid he'll go too far one day, and he'll…" Tears began to fall down her cheeks.

"Kill you? My dear girl, that just won't do." Miss Bethany came around to her and hugged her tight. "As it happens, I have a young gent from Dayton Falls looking for a bride."

"Dayton Falls? Where Miss Charlotte is living?" Joy filled her heart. She would be reunited with her dear Charlotte.

Miss Bethany grinned at her. "I do have other gentlemen on the books as well, but not from Dayton Falls. Your choice entirely."

Allie was certain Miss Bethany already knew her answer, but she told her anyway. "I'll take him."

Miss Bethany was on her feet in seconds. "No," she said, shaking her head. "It doesn't work that way. You have to read his letter, *then* make your decision." She shoved a letter toward the younger woman.

As Allie read the letter, Miss Bethany pulled out four more letters. "It is customary to read at least five letters, then decide."

She handed those letters over to Allie, who waved them away. "You can pretend I read them," she said cheekily. "I'll take this man." She pointed at the letter. "The barber." She looked up at Miss Bethany. "It's not as exotic as a sheriff, but he does sound nice."

The other woman nodded. "We'll organise a letter to go back to him."

Allie stood. "I have to do this quickly. I can't risk going back to work; I could be dead tomorrow."

The two women stood. "Get your things together, Allie," she said. "I will do for you what I did for Miss Charlotte. Take the train in the morning, and I'll send him a telegram to meet you at the station."

Chapter Two

Allie was prepared for the long journey after what Charlotte had told her.

Stealing through the partly-lit street was nothing new for her – she did it every day since she began work at the crack of dawn and didn't finish until after sunset. She was a servant in every sense.

Charlie Jones, the barber from Dayton Falls, had written he needed a wife to keep his house clean, cook meals, and help him out in his barber shop in town.

She didn't think he was anywhere near as rich as the Montgomery's – they were filthy rich – but she didn't think he was dirt poor, either.

Somewhere in between perhaps.

And she just bet he was handsome. And tall.

She lay back on the carriage seat dreamily thinking about her new husband-to-be. Hopefully he would be at the station when she arrived. She didn't want to be alone for too long.

She glanced down at her dress. Would he be disappointed that her clothes weren't of the same caliber as Charlotte's?

She was a mere servant compared to Charlotte's high standing in the community.

The train whistle sounded – they were pulling into Dayton Falls. She looked herself over again. She'd washed her face, brushed down her clothes, and pulled her hair together the best she could under the circumstances.

She unfolded the piece of paper screwed up in her hands. She'd been grasping it tightly since before she boarded the train. "Charlie Jones," she said quietly. "Charlie Jones."

She had rehearsed his name over and over during the long and grueling days on the train. Surely she wouldn't forget it now?

As the train ground to a halt, she grabbed her well-worn bag with her meagre belongings and bolted from the train. She didn't want to stay a moment longer than was necessary.

She almost knocked over a well-dressed man on the platform. "Charlie Jones?" she asked, nearly toppling him.

"No Ma'am," he said, and went on his way. She tightened the grip on her bag.

She stood planted to the spot for about fifteen minutes, then heard the conductor and began to panic. "All aboard!" he roared, as the train was getting ready to leave again.

"Allie!" She turned to a familiar voice, and much-loved face.

"Oh, Miss Charlotte," she said, tears streaming down her face.

The two embraced, they were so happy to see each other. She didn't see the little group behind Miss Charlotte to begin with.

Charlotte stepped back. "Allie, this is my husband, Sheriff Angus Doyle, and our children."

Angus tipped his hat. "Please to meet you, Ma'am."

"And this smiling gentleman is Charlie Jones."

He stepped forward. "I am very pleased to meet you, Ma'am," he said, fiddling with his hands as though he didn't know what to do with them.

As Allie turned toward her groom-to-be, Charlotte called her out. "What is that, that… on your face?" she asked quietly. She held Allie's face and had a good look. "Oh my goodness, Allie. How did you get that bruise?"

Allie stared at the ground. "I shouldn't say."

Charlotte's eyes opened wide. "Did my father do this? Is that why you wanted to leave?" She pulled Allie close to her and hugged her. "I'm so sorry," she whispered, her voice breaking.

"Please don't tell anyone," Allie whispered.

Charlotte nodded, sadness on her face. "Well," she said more cheerfully, "You're in the right place. Welcome to your new and better life." She looked across to her husband and smiled. "I love it here, and I know you will too."

Charlie reached forward and took the bag from Allie's hands. "Let me take that, Miss Allie." He put his arm behind her to guide her out of the train station. "You must be very tired after your long journey."

Charlie Jones seemed like a nice man. A gentleman. Someone she could perhaps come to love over time.

"I am a little," she said. "But not so much we can't go and get married right now if that's what you want."

She watched as his face went from wary to beaming in a matter of seconds. "Yes, Ma'am," he said, then scooped her up and spun her around.

Her arms went around his neck, and she whispered in his ear. "Charlie," she said quietly. "Unless you want to wear my breakfast, I suggest you stop flinging me about, and put me down gently."

She couldn't wait to marry this man. Life promised to be interesting from now on.

* * *

"And do you take this woman, to be your lawfully wed wife," the preacher asked.

Charlie stared down at his new bride and smiled. "I surely do, Preacher," he said.

"I now pronounce you man and wife." He looked from one to the other of them. "You may now kiss your bride, Charlie."

Allie's eyes opened wide, and he stared at her. Should he kiss her? Right here in the church? But those lips looked so darned kissable, and he couldn't resist.

He studied her face. She was ever so pretty. Her brown hair had sun streaks through it, and it glistened under the sunlight. He'd noticed it on their way to the church.

And her eyes. He could get lost in those mournful mushroom colored eyes. She seemed to have a sadness about her.

A sadness that he intended to rid from her.

Charlie held her face with both hands and leaned down close to her face. He slowly moved in and brushed his lips against hers.

She tasted sweet like red wine, and he wanted more. He glanced at her eyes. *She looked kinda scared. Was he scaring her? He sure hoped not.*

He stood up. "I'm sorry," he whispered. "I shouldn't have done that."

She licked her freshly kissed lips. "You're my husband. You're entitled," she said softly, so only he could hear.

He wondered what she was really thinking. Was she annoyed at him? She didn't look annoyed, but she didn't look happy either.

There were a small handful of town people in the congregation, including Charlotte and her family.

Mrs Jensen, Mrs Green, and Mrs Jackson were also there, along with Mrs Foggerty who owned the only boarding house in town.

The man who started it all, the one who took the first mail order bride was also there – Pete from the Post Office, along with his lovely bride.

The bride and groom made their way back out of the church, followed by everyone else.

Charlotte was grinning from ear to ear, and Charlie was happy. The fact the two women were friends meant his new bride may not get so homesick.

Allie stood there, surrounded by strangers, but it didn't seem to faze her. She was smiling and reached for his hand. Whether that was because she liked him, or for reassurance he wasn't sure, but he'd take all he could get at this point.

"I'm so happy for you, Allie," Charlotte said, hugging her friend. "And you too, of course, Charlie." She turned to him. "I just know you will be as happy as Angus and I are."

She squeezed her friend tight again, then stepped back and threw rice over the two of them.

"Congratulations, my dears," Mrs Foggerty said. Charlie wasn't in the least surprised to see the elderly lady here. She attended every wedding that was held in Dayton Falls. She was a town icon.

"There's a small reception at our place," Charlotte said. "You know the way, Charlie."

He looked down at his bride. She was shivering. He pulled off his jacket and draped it across her shoulders. "You're cold," he said. "I can't have my bride cold on her wedding day." He pulled her close to his side and tried to warm her up.

He hoped today was the beginning of a happy life for both of them.

* * *

It was late afternoon by the time they got back to Charlie's place.

Charlotte had put on a lovely reception for them. It must have been a lot of work for her, and Allie really appreciated the effort she'd gone to.

But now she was home. Her home for the rest of her life.

She swallowed hard.

Had she really fled her family home and traveled for days to marry a perfect stranger? She imagined Charlotte had the same thoughts go through her mind when she arrived. And look at her now. She and Angus seemed perfectly happy. Blissful even.

They even had a brood of offspring. The thought made Allie melancholy. Would she and Charlie end up like that?

She certainly hoped so.

"Let me take your bag," she heard Charlie say. After dropping her bag to the ground, he held her around the waist and lifted her off the wagon.

She stared down into his face, taking in clear blue eyes, and his long blond lashes. They matched his hair perfectly.

When he pulled his hat off his head, she'd noticed the kink in his hair. It was just a tiny curl, but it was there, and it was endearing.

A lock of hair fell over his face, and she wanted to reach out and push it back. But they'd only known each other a matter of hours, and she didn't want to appear forward. That just wouldn't do.

Oh no! He'd noticed her staring and stared right back into her big brown eyes. She felt the heat creep up her face.

She'd used make up to try and cover the bruise, but Charlotte had spotted it anyway. She hoped that Charlie didn't, but wondered how long she would manage to disguise it.

She sighed.

She was about to start her new life as a young wife, in a town that was very new to her.

Her feet gently touched the ground. "This is home," Charlie said, grabbing her belongings off the ground.

He walked her to the front door and opened it. Suddenly she was lifted off the ground.

"What the....?"

He had one arm under her legs, and the other around her. She slid her arms around his neck so she didn't fall.

"I'm carrying you over the threshold," he said, hurt in his voice. "Don't you know brides should be carried over the threshold into their bridal home?"

She laughed. "I'd surely forgotten," she said, joy in her heart. Charlie seemed to be a bit of a softie.

Once again, he put her down gently, then closed the door behind him after scooping up her bag again.

"It's not much, but it's comfortable," he told her.

She looked about. There were a few chairs scattered about and a big fireplace, with a box of wood next to it. Next to the chairs stood a low table, and on the table was a lantern. Ready for the evening no doubt.

"Follow me," Charlie said. So she did. "This is my bedroom," he motioned her to go in. She stood at the doorway and stared hesitantly into the room.

There was a big double bed, with a small wardrobe for clothes, and a cupboard beside the bed. On the bed was a beautiful comforter, made with patchwork. Someone had spent many hours putting it together.

Allie sighed. She wished she was so talented.

"My mother made it," he said, startling her out of her thoughts. "I've had it for some years."

She nodded. "It's very beautiful," she told him. It wasn't a lie.

He put his hand to her back and guided her toward another room. "This will be your room," he said, putting her belongings in a corner of the room.

She nodded, but inwardly was disappointed. He'd just assumed she didn't want to be his wife in every way, only a wife in name? She'd known from the start he wanted a wife to look after the house and help at his barber shop when needed. So why was she upset?

Her eyes filled with tears, but she fought them back. She couldn't let him see how upset she was. She thought Charlie Jones had wanted a wife, but what he really wanted was a servant.

She hadn't progressed at all. Just moved from one servant's position to another.

She hoped that down the track he would regard her more highly? Even invite her to his bed. She wasn't sure, but for now this had to do.

At least here she was safe. Her hand flew to her face. The memory of it made it feel like her cheek had just been struck by Mr Montgomery.

It was her imagination of course, but she was reliving that moment all over again.

Charlie seemed like a kind man, someone who would never hurt her. She turned to him and studied his face. She was certain she was safe here with him. Charlotte would have warned her otherwise.

"Thank you, Charlie," she said softly, then took off his jacket and handed it to him. "Perhaps show me the kitchen now, so I can prepare your lunch."

He took the jacket from her hands, and grinned. She knew exactly why Charlie needed a wife.

Chapter Three

Charlie awoke to delicious smells coming from the kitchen.

His kitchen that now had a woman in it.

Now he would get decent meals instead of cold beans most nights. He occasionally deviated by having hot beans, and on the odd occasion he made fried eggs. But that was as far as his cooking skills went.

But he got married yesterday to a pretty little thing who made delicious food. Last night's lunch was the best he'd had for a very long time. His mouth near watered thinking about it.

It stuck in his mind it had taken all his effort to get her to sit down at the table with him, and even to eat.

Something had obviously happened to Allie at some point, because she was very flighty. She cringed when he went near her and kept an eye on him the entire time.

He climbed out of bed, and headed for the kitchen, but suddenly remembered he was no longer alone in the house. He didn't want to appear indecent in front of his new bride.

He pulled his robe up around his shoulders and stood in the doorway of the kitchen watching his new bride prepare his breakfast.

Those pancakes smelled delicious. He knew he was going to enjoy being a married man. He'd prayed for a wonderful woman to marry, and his prayers had been answered.

He felt a little guilty that he'd also asked for a good cook but couldn't help himself. It was really a necessity.

He stood there silently taking in her every feature. The tiny little waist, and her perfect profile. Her long blonde hair was tied back in a loose plait, and he longed to touch it. To touch her.

But that wasn't part of the agreement.

He'd asked for a wife to take care of his house and help with his barber shop. He had no right to ask for anything more. Or indeed to expect more. But he couldn't help thinking about it.

She turned around to place the hot pancakes on the table and was startled. "Oh my gosh," she said. "I didn't see you there."

Charlie stood straighter in the doorway. "I'm sorry," he said, meaning every word. "I was intrigued to watch you cook. I didn't mean to startle you."

She nodded, and continued putting the food on the table, then turned back to get his coffee. "Sit down and eat," she said. "How do you have your coffee?"

Charlie dug in. "Strong and black," he said between mouthfuls. "This is good. " he said. "Really good."

She placed his coffee in front of him. "Sit," he said. "I don't want to eat alone. I've done that for far too long."

She looked shocked but nodded.

He noticed she'd only set the table for one. She pulled another plate and cutlery from the cupboard.

"Allie," he said, feeling his face stiffen. "You are my wife. We eat together. Always."

She nodded again but didn't look convinced.

He wasn't sure what the problem was but was determined to get to the bottom of it. He watched carefully as she slowly sat down at the table and took just one pancake. He leaned forward to pile more on her plate, and she flinched.

As though she thought he would strike her.

He felt as though he'd been struck down himself. "Allie," he said quietly. "Is there a problem?"

She shook her head and continued to eat. He noticed she didn't have coffee and got up from the table and poured one for her. When he leaned across to place it in front of her, she jumped up from her chair, and out of his reach.

"What's going on, Allie," he asked quietly. "What are you afraid of?"

She studied him through half closed eyes. "Nothing," she said, far too quickly for his liking.

He pulled her close to him. She felt warm and soft, and his heart rate quickened just having her near. His arms went up around her without his consent, and she rested her head on his chest.

Then just as quickly she pulled away. "I, I have to clean up," she said, pulling out of his grip.

His eyes bore into her. "No, no you don't. I want to hold my wife. Is that alright?" He didn't wait for an answer, just pulled her to him again.

It felt so right. They'd known each other less than twenty-four hours, but this felt so good, as though they were always meant to be together.

Through the fog of bliss, his thoughts went back to her reaction. Someone had harmed her, he was certain of it.

And he wanted to find out who. "Who hurt you, Allie?" He hadn't meant to blurt it out, but spoke slightly above a whisper, as though a gentle voice might entice her to tell him.

She looked up at him with those big brown eyes he could get lost in. Then her eyes began to fill with tears. She blinked them back, but it didn't work, they began to roll down her cheeks.

He lifted his fingers and brushed her warm tears aside. As he did so, the make up on her face began to wipe away and he saw the purple bruise on her delicate skin.

Fury began to bubble up inside of him. Who would do such a thing to a gentle soul like Allie? His whole body stiffened at the thought.

She obviously didn't want to talk about it. "I understand," he said quietly, and brushed his hands across her back.

She pulled out of his grip and sat down once more. "You'd better eat up," she said quietly, as though nothing had happened. "You'll be late for work."

He lifted his coffee to his mouth and studied her over the mug. Who was this woman who sat opposite him, and what had happened to her to cause her harm?

At least now he knew why she needed to get away from Westlake in such a hurry. He was more endeared to her each time he saw her.

She took small mouthfuls of pancake as she watched him watching her. There could be interesting times ahead.

* * *

After checking out the pantry, Allie went to the Mercantile as Charlie had instructed.

Charlie's house was situated behind the Barber's Shop. Something Allie had not realized previously. Which meant it was just a short stroll to the Mercantile, only a few minutes away.

He'd told her to put everything on his account and get whatever she needed. That included new dresses for herself.

Apart from one other dress and some delicates she'd quickly shoved in her bag before she left, Allie had arrived in the clothes she stood up in.

As she strolled across the dirt road to the store, she lifted her skirts and adjusted her bonnet. As Charlie's new bride, she needed to make a good impression.

She stepped up to the counter full of confidence. "Mr Horvard?" she asked the man who stood there looking at her curiously.

"Yes," he said warily. "That's me."

"I'm Charlie Jones' new bride. He told me I should introduce myself, and to tell you to put everything on his account."

Mr Horvard's eyes lit up. She was certain his brain was ticking over with dollar signs.

She sighed.

"I need to replenish the pantry," she said. "It's almost bare." She checked the list she'd made before leaving the house. "I'll need flour, eggs, and milk, as well as potatoes and beans."

In future they would buy their eggs from Charlotte and Angus, but right now, she needed more.

"Oh, and I need dresses. Do you sell those, or is there a dress shop in town?"

Mr Horvard frowned. "I sell every day dresses, but if you want gowns, then you'll need to visit the dress shop at the other end of town." He pointed out the dress stand at the back of the shop.

"Do you wish to help yourself, Mrs Jones," he asked. "Or would you like some assistance?"

Mrs Jones. It rolled of the tongue nicely. It was usually Allie giving assistance to others, so it was a nice change to receive some herself.

She smiled at the man watching her intensely. "Your assistance would be very appreciated, Mr Horvard," she said. "I'm not sure I'll be able to manage alone."

He nodded and reached for a wooden box. "Where would you like to start Mrs Jones?"

He followed Allie around like a lost puppy while she added the necessary items to the box. "I'll go and check out the dresses now, if you don't mind," she said. "Perhaps while you tally my other items?"

The store owner nodded and returned to the front counter.

Allie checked out the dresses. The first one on the stand was made of white calico. She pushed that aside – it reminded her too much of the plain dresses she had been forced to wear as a servant to the Montgomery's.

As she worked her way through the dresses on offer, she found two that caught her attention. She didn't need anything fancy, but she would like to look pretty for her new husband. Something that might catch his eye.

The first dress was beige with tiny flowers all over it. She loved the floral pattern and was certain the color would suit her.

The next one was plaid with browns and reds and a touch of yellow. She held it up against herself. It was a pity there wasn't a mirror for her to check her reflection.

"Good morning, Mrs Jones." It was Mrs Jensen from the auxiliary. She'd been at the church for the wedding.

"A good morning to you too, Mrs Jensen. I am choosing some new dresses." She held the plaid one in front of her. "What do you think of this one? Does it suit my coloring?"

The older woman beamed. "It most certainly does my dear. Now hold the other one up." She took the plaid dress from Allie's hands. "That is perfect as well. Our dear Charlie is going to love them."

She winked, and Allie felt the heat creep up her face. Why she felt embarrassment, she didn't know. Being married was very new to her, so that must be it.

"I had to get supplies to make Charlie's supper," she said, heading for the counter. "I had best get a move on."

"Yes, of course. I'll see you at church on Sunday?"

"Absolutely," Allie said. "I couldn't bear to miss it." She gave the other woman a quick hug and went to collect her purchases.

The store was filling up. "Are you here alone, Mr Horvard? You look like you could use some help."

He gazed at her thoughtfully, then laughed. "Yes to both," he said. "I should get myself a wife to help me out."

Allie wondered if he knew she was a mail order bride. She felt her face go red and put her hands to her cheeks.

"Thank you Mr Horvard," she said, struggling through the door with her purchases. "I will see you next time."

She wondered exactly how many people knew. She hadn't thought about the embarrassment she would feel being known as a mail order bride.

But she was thick-skinned enough to realize her safety was more important than her reputation. After all, she'd endured years of torment from people knowing she was a lowly servant.

Chapter Four

Charlie swept the hair off the floor of his Barber's Shop.

He'd watched his wife stroll over to the Mercantile. He'd also watched her look around, as if making sure it was safe to do so.

She'd come from a big town, and he would have put it down to that if he hadn't seen the bruise on her face.

That made her actions more sinister.

Not on her part, but definitely on the part of the person whose hands she'd suffered from.

He wanted to run to her and hold her tight. To protect her from whatever invisible element she was afraid of.

Instead, he stood in the doorway watching her cross the road.

Business was slow today. So far he'd only had one customer, but he didn't mind. That was all he needed to keep him going.

He scratched his head. Now that he had a wife, he should probably aim higher.

He continued to stare across the road to the Mercantile, and watched Mrs Jensen arrive. A few minutes later, his Allie came out, struggling with a big box of items.

He threw the broom aside and rushed to help her. "Let me," he said, when he was almost next to her.

"But, your shop…"

He looked down into her beautiful brown eyes. "Nonsense," he said. "There are no customers right now, so it's fine."

He snatched the box away from her, and carried it across the road and into the house. He lifted the dresses. "These are pretty," he said, smiling at her. "Just like you."

She stared at him and he laughed. "I love it when your cheeks go pink."

Her hands flew to her face, but he pulled them down. "Don't cover your beauty," he said. "I love your pretty face."

He leaned into her, and lightly kissed her lips. "I have to go now," he said, frowning. "I wish I could stay."

Allie finally found her voice. "Thank you. For carrying the box for me, I mean."

He tipped his hat to her and left without another word.

Allie packed away her purchases and began to make a stew for supper.

Once the stew was cooking, her stomach began to rumble.

She'd put on a thick vegetable soup earlier and made biscuits for Charlie's lunch. He shut up shop at half past noon exactly he'd told her, and then would be in for lunch.

He was true to his word.

"Sit down." Allie put a mug of coffee in front of him. "Strong and black."

She turned her back and dished up the hot soup, then proceeded to place it in front of him too.

A plate of biscuits was left in the middle of the table, along with butter.

Charlie's mouth was already full. "This is magnificent," he said with his mouth half-full. "I feel like a king at a feast." He grinned, and it went all the way to his twinkling blue eyes.

"I never imagined I would end up with an amazing cook for a wife."

Allie joined him at the table and watched as he filled his belly with her cooking. "I'm not that good of a cook," she said.

He stared at her. "I'm giving you a compliment, Allie," he said. "Can you not just accept it?"

Her bottom lip quivered, and she had to rein herself in. "No one has ever complimented me before," she said quietly.

"What the hell…?" Charlie was on his feet and shoved his chair back. It scraped across the floor and the noise went through her head.

She cringed and closed her eyes tightly. It was her natural defense mechanism she'd used to brace herself against Mr Montgomery.

She gasped when she felt his touch. But it wasn't harsh like the Master, it was gentle, and he wrapped his arms around her and pulled her close.

His lips lightly kissed her forehead, then he rubbed his hands across her back.

"Tell me, Allie," he said gently. His voice was soft and caring.

She swallowed hard and looked up into his face. "I, I can't."

He frowned at her but tightened his hold on her. "I'll protect you," he said softly. "I'm your husband. I won't let anyone hurt you."

"There's no one to protect me from," she said roughly, and pulled out of his grip. She wasn't lying. Now that she was here in Dayton Falls, she was safe from the Master. "Sit down and finish your food. It's nearly time to open the shop again."

He stared at her, and she wondered what he was thinking. Did he already regret marrying her? Would he get an annulment? Because surely this marriage wasn't turning out the way he'd expected.

Allie swallowed back a sob and forced herself to eat her soup.

* * *

Charlie couldn't sleep.

He'd tossed and turned until the early hours of the morning, then finally got up to make himself a snack.

Perhaps that would help.

But he knew it wouldn't. The thing that was bothering him was Allie. The way she flinched if he moved too quickly toward her. The bruise on her face, and her sub-servient behavior.

He could ask Charlotte Doyle. They were friends, she could tell him what was going on.

He scratched his head as he sat at the kitchen table, with the moonlight providing the only light to their homely kitchen.

No. He couldn't do that. Asking Charlotte would be asking her to break a confidence. He shouldn't put her in that position.

His belly rumbled. Charlie had no idea why, because his belly was fuller than it had ever been.

His mouth near drooled at the thought of Allie's creations, and he wondered if there was any left-over cake in the pantry.

He lit a lantern and silently slipped into the pantry. His eyes gravitated to a tin in the far corner. This was it, he was sure.

A nice slice of chocolate cake with coffee would go down a treat.

He returned to the kitchen and loaded the stove with wood, ready for the morning. It was rather chilly this time of year, and it wouldn't hurt to have the stove fired up overnight.

He bent over to light the fire. It would help to heat up the coffee too.

Everything he did reminded him of his beautiful wife, but he didn't know how to mend her worries.

After the fire had ignited, he picked up the lantern and headed for Allie's room. He felt compelled to watch her sleep.

Did that make him some sort of deviant?

He thought not, because he was her husband. He was concerned about her safety and wanted to ensure she was safely tucked up in bed.

He stood in the doorway with the lantern half in the room, half out. He didn't want to cause so much light it disturbed her, but he wanted to assure himself she was alright.

He stood and watched her for a few minutes.

She lay on her side facing the wall. Her long blonde hair was draped over the pillow, and her hands tucked in underneath the comforter.

But he was drawn to her face.

It was relaxed in sleep, but not during the day, he noticed. He was seeing a totally different person as she slept.

He took a couple of steps forward; he wanted to see her beautiful face. Charlie watched her breathing, deep and slowly, just like he'd imagined.

He took another step toward her and her eyes opened wide.

She began to scream long and loud.

He'd frightened her, and now she was terrified.

He put down the lantern and tried to calm her, but it only served to make things worse.

She was kicking and screaming. Her arms were flailing all over the place, and at one point she almost punched him in the face.

"Allie. Allie!" he yelled. "It's just me, Charlie." He pulled her close to him and wrapped her tightly in his arms.

He sat on the bed with her pulled into his lap. This woman, his wife, needed him. By the looks of things, she needed him as much as he needed her. But for totally different reasons.

He rocked back and forth with her on his lap until she calmed down.

"I'm sorry," she whispered in the cold night air, her eyes tightly closed.

He pulled her closer still. "No, it is I who should be sorry," he said quietly. "I'm the one who caused this distress."

She opened her eyes and stared up at him. Every time he looked at them, they seemed a different color. Tonight they looked like copper. Yesterday they'd looked more like mushrooms, and last night they were closer to sepia.

They were fascinating, like the woman herself.

"I got up for a snack," he confessed. "I raided the pantry." He gave her a weak smile. "But then I felt compelled to come and check on you."

Her hand went to his cheek. "That was sweet. Thank you."

She rested her head against his chest and sighed.

"I think I'm alright now," she whispered. "I, I just got a fright."

He frowned. "No, you didn't. Something else is going on." He reached for her hand and squeezed it. "I'm your husband, Allie. You can tell me anything."

She nodded her head, but he wasn't assured. He worried for his wife.

"I lit the fire," he said, trying to distract her. "Do you want coffee?" She shook her head. "Tea?"

She agreed and pulled her gown around herself. He walked with her to the kitchen where he sat her at the table. The kettle had heated enough for tea, and he poured her a drink.

She grinned at the empty cake tin sitting on the table. "I guess I'll make more tomorrow," she said.

But she wasn't angry, he was sure. She seemed happy he'd eaten her cake. Or perhaps satisfied was a better description.

He sat opposite her and reached for Allie's hand. It was tiny. And soft.

She didn't pull it away.

"Do you want to talk about it?"

She licked her lips and opened her mouth to speak, then snapped it shut again. She shook her head. "Not tonight. Maybe some other time?"

He took a sip of his coffee. "When you're ready," he told her. His gut told him she was in deep trouble, but his heart hoped he was wrong.

* * *

Allie woke up wrapped in the arms of her husband.

Sleep had evaded her after their rendezvous in the kitchen, and she'd begun to wander the house. Still wide awake, Charlie convinced her to lay on top of his bed.

He'd been so kind, and gentle, and they lay together quietly for a long time. After a while they'd both become cold and had climbed under the comforter.

"I promise not to do anything to you," he'd said, and she'd agreed. Charlie would never break her trust, she was certain.

It hadn't taken long, and she finally fell asleep in his arms. She was so exhausted from the events of earlier.

And here she was now, still wrapped in his arms.

Allie needed to slip out of the bed without waking him. She had work to do; make Charlie's breakfast, fix the fire, and put on the coffee.

She slipped soundlessly out of bed, Charlie's bed, and pulled her robe up around herself.

The fire was still burning from when it had been lit overnight but needed replenishing. She silently thanked her husband for lighting the fire in the early hours. It made the kitchen so much warmer than the previous day.

She had left over bread from the previous evening's meal and sliced it thickly. She put butter and honey on the table and set two places.

Taking the frying pan from the cupboard, she threw in slices of bacon to cook, and had the eggs at the ready. They wouldn't take long to cook once Charlie was up and about.

She had two mugs lined up on the counter waiting for the mugs to boil, then sat at the table while she waited.

"Good morning wife of mine," Charlie said with a grin as he entered the kitchen. "Something smells amazing." He leaned into Allie and kissed her cheek. "How are you feeling this morning?"

She loved the way he cared about her. "I'm perfectly fine," she said. "Thanks for asking."

He sat at the head of the table where he always sat and waited for his coffee to be served. Allie stared at him.

He looked particularly handsome today. Was it the clothes he was wearing? She loved those brown breeches worn with his white shirt and waistcoat. She thought he was a little over-dressed for work but had no intentions of telling him.

She stood thoughtfully while she waited for the eggs to fry and wondered if it was perhaps the way he'd helped her last night.

Honestly, she wasn't sure. What she did know was that everything had changed for her. She no longer felt like an intruder in her new husband's home but felt a little more like she belonged.

Perhaps over time she'd feel like she really did belong?

She pulled two plates out of the cupboard, adding six slices of bacon and two eggs to Charlie's plate, and much less to her own.

He protested loudly. "You need to eat more, Allie," he argued. "Take some of mine – you are far too thin to be healthy."

She declined but reveled in watching him enjoy every mouthful.

"I swear I'll be double the size by the end of the month," he said, wiping his mouth with a napkin.

He gulped down the last of his coffee. "That was delicious, and now I have to go to work." He came to her once more and kissed her cheek, and then he was gone.

Allie sipped her tea and finished off her breakfast, then planned out her day in her head. She decided to make a roast for supper and checked the pantry for supplies.

Convinced everything she needed was there, she cleaned the kitchen and began to prepare the roast, then put it in the oven.

She threw more wood on the fire, then prepared pea soup for Charlie's lunch. She made a batch of cheese biscuits as well. He seemed to like those very much.

This afternoon she would make a pound cake.

Right now though, she needed to clean the kitchen. She swept the floor, and washed it, then pottered around the rest of the house, cleaning here and there, and putting everything in its place.

Not that it was dirty or untidy, but she could see why Charlie would need a wife to help him out. It would be a big job for a man who was also trying to run business.

She startled when Charlie came rushing through the door, and her heart rate beat up. That was because he surprised her, right?

"I'm sorry I'm late," he said. "I had a customer, and I couldn't send him away because the missus had lunch waiting."

He gave her a weak smile, and she grinned.

"Of course you couldn't. Sit down then." She waved him to sit and dished out his lunch.

"Oooh, pea soup," he said excitedly. "I haven't had pea soup for years. You certainly know the way to a man's heart."

Allie did want to reach his heart, but she hoped food wasn't going to be how she got there.

Chapter Five

Charlie found himself getting up in the night more and more.

For no other reason than he heard Allie cry out, and sometimes she screamed, and it bothered him. And sometimes she made no sound at all.

No matter, it had become a habit to get up and check on her.

When it was really bad, he'd bring her back to his bed where he could comfort her, and settle her back down to sleep.

It helped him as well. Knowing she was safe in his arms, seemed to put him into a deep sleep.

Some days he would wake to find her gone, and other days she'd still be there, wrapped in his arms, just the way he liked it.

Today though, she was there, still in a very deep sleep.

He kissed her on the neck, trying to wake her up gently.

"Allie," he whispered. "Time to wake up."

She rolled toward him, and her eyes fluttered open. "Morning, husband," she said, a weak smile on her face.

He leaned in and kissed her lightly. "I love when you call me husband," he said softly, touching her cheek with his fingers.

"I love when you call me wife."

They stared at each other for long minutes. "I'd better get breakfast started," she finally said, climbing out of the warm bed.

She pulled her robe around herself and was about to leave the room when Charlie called her back. "Allie, come here." She turned around and found herself face to face with her husband, who was standing at the side of the bed.

His arms went up around her, and his hands cupped her face. "I know we haven't known each other all that long," he said. "but I really care for you, Allie," he said, running his hand down the side of her neck. "I can't believe I'm saying this, but," he stared into her beautiful brown eyes, mesmerized by them, and flicked back a stray piece of blonde hair. "I really miss you when I'm at work."

Her eyes opened wide and she stared up into his face. "I miss you too," she whispered. He wondered if she was telling the truth, or just saying it to appease him.

He leaned into her and gently kissed her lips, lingering longer than he should. Still, it wasn't enough. He wanted more, much more. Probably more than Allie was willing to give.

This was his fault.

After all, he's the one that wanted a wife in name only. Now he had to live with that.

* * *

Allie thought about what Charlie had said to her this morning. About how he cared for her, and how he missed her when she wasn't there.

She felt a tingle down her spine. She felt exactly the same way about him.

They hadn't been together all that long, but it was long enough that she'd developed feelings for him.

He was a nice person, a caring person, and she felt safe when he was around. Knowing his Barber Shop was on the other side of the wall was like having him there with her. Only he wasn't.

She was particularly missing him this morning. Maybe because he'd held her so tenderly this morning? Or perhaps it was the way he'd lingered when he kissed her.

It might even have been the way his hands caressed her.

She really didn't know, but it made her feel special.

No one had ever made her feel that way before. She smiled. She wanted to do something special for Charlie. Sort of like repaying his kindness toward her.

She pulled a mug out of the cupboard and poured a coffee – just the way he liked it. Then she reached for the cake tin. She still had some pound cake left, so cut a big chunk for her Charlie.

She laughed. He would get such a surprise when she took it too him.

He was always so hungry when he came in for lunch, and this would tide him over.

Allie removed her apron, picked up her offerings and went around to the shop. But she hadn't thought about the fact her hands would be full, and she couldn't open the door.

She stood there struggling until Charlie noticed her. The look on his face was priceless when he opened the door and saw what she'd brought for him.

He held the door open while she walked through, putting the cake and coffee on the counter. Then she glanced around.

He had a customer in the chair, half shaved, and another two waiting. It was a busy day for Charlie, which meant he'd probably be very late for lunch.

"I, I didn't mean to disturb you," she apologized, and turned to leave.

He put down the razor in his hand and called her back. "You didn't," he said. "It was a wonderful surprise. Thank you."

"Who's the pretty lady?" It was the customer in the chair, who was patiently waiting.

"This is my new wife, Allie," he said to the room. "So don't none of you boys go getting any ideas."

She heard a low whistle. "How did you manage to nab such a beauty," the man said, then began to laugh.

It annoyed Allie greatly. She reached for Charlie, and put her arms around his neck, pulling him in for a kiss. Only she didn't expect Charlie to react quite so vigorously.

He grinned at her as he pulled back. "Off with you woman, before you give me ideas," he said with a grin, and slapped Allie on the butt.

She scampered away before he said anything even more embarrassing.

* * *

Allie stood in the doorway, holding tight to Charlie's hand.

She'd never been to a dance before and had no idea what to expect.

She looked around the room, taking in the couples on the dance floor, as well as the many lone men standing on the perimeter. The music was loud, and she could barely hear when Charlie spoke to her.

As she continued gazing around, she spotted the table where she needed to leave her contribution of food for the night.

Before she could move, Mrs Jensen, came scurrying toward her. "I'll take that from you, my dear," she shouted. It was almost impossible to hear over the ruckus otherwise.

Allie nodded, and Charlie squeezed her hand. "Wanna dance?" he asked loudly.

She leaned into him and spoke into his ear. "I don't know how." But he took her hand and led her onto the dance floor anyway.

The music was almost overpowering, but Charlie pushed forward. He took one of her hands in his, and wrapped the other around her back, then pulled her close.

She leaned her head on his chest and relaxed into him. They shuffled around the floor, almost to the beat of the music – Charlie was as bad at dancing as she was, but he didn't care. And while she was with him, she wasn't going to worry either.

She felt as though she was in heaven, being there with her husband. Being held so close. At times it felt almost indecent being held this way out in public for everyone to see. But Charlie insisted.

No one else was dancing this way, they were mostly all doing the waltz, and eventually she pulled away from him. "I need to sit down for a while," she said. She hated to lie to her husband, but Charlie wouldn't take no for an answer.

She'd met some of the local ladies at church last Sunday and as she rested, she looked around. She only saw a few unfamiliar faces. Hopefully she'd get to meet some of them.

"Allie! I'm so glad you came." Charlotte leaned down and hugged her tight. Angus was there too, watching their children while their mother spoke with her.

Allie hugged her back. "I'm so glad to see you," she said.

"How are you settling in? Tell me all about it." Charlotte stood back waiting for her answer.

There wasn't much to tell. "Everything is going fine. Charlie's a wonderful man, and I'm very fond of him," she told her friend.

She watched as Charlie stood beside Angus, and the two men chatted.

"He's treating you well?"

"He's a real gentleman," Allie said. "I couldn't have asked for a better husband."

Her heartbeat quickened as he strolled toward her, looking very dapper in his Sunday best and his big black Stetson. When he reached out and touched her hand, a tingle went down her spine.

"Shall we dance?" he asked.

Allie wanted nothing more than to hear her husband's heart beat and they danced arm in arm.

* * *

"That was fun, even if I can't dance," she said when they arrived home.

Allie put the kettle on for a midnight supper. She pulled the cake tin out of the pantry and cut a piece for Charlie. Her stomach was overloaded from the variety of fare available at the dance, so she refrained.

"Your pound cake was very popular," Charlie told her. "There wasn't even a crumb left." He gulped his coffee when it was put in front of him.

She grinned. She'd never thought of herself as a good cook until she'd come to Dayton Falls. She'd helped cook out from time to time, but that was it.

Her limited skills were getting a good work out now though. It helped that some of the local women had shared their recipes with her.

"Yours is the best coffee I've ever had," he said, taking another big mouthful.

"It's just coffee. Nothing special about it."

"Come here, wife of mine," he said, motioning her toward him. When Allie arrived, he pulled her into his lap.

His arms quickly went around her. "Did you enjoy yourself tonight? It looked like you did."

She relaxed against him. "I did. It was a lot of fun. More fun than I've ever had before."

She felt him stiffen against her. "Do you want to tell me why you had to run away?" he asked softly. "It seems your life has been difficult, if not dangerous."

She shook her head. Now was not the time. But she couldn't envisage a time she would ever want to tell her husband she had had been an abused servant in a rich man's house. It was humiliating, even if it hadn't been her fault.

* * *

It had been almost three weeks since Allie had arrived, and they still slept in separate rooms. Although, surprisingly, Allie sometimes crept into his bed during the night.

He didn't complain.

He would hold her tight, his arms wrapped around her.

Tonight was one of those nights.

She silently slid into his bed, placing the lantern on the dresser, then tucked herself up against him. Charlie pulled her close and snuggled into her.

"Having trouble sleeping again?" Whatever had been bothering her when she arrived, still worried her. Every now and then she had nightmares. He always heard her.

He wanted to go to her, to hold her in his arms and make everything right again.

But he couldn't, not without her permission.

He hadn't asked for a wife in all ways, he'd asked for a wife to clean his house and cook his meals. What right did he have to change those terms? In short, he didn't.

Allie had made it abundantly clear she was willing to do those chores and leave it at that. He hoped that one day they could become husband and wife in every way.

But he was certain it wouldn't happen any day soon.

"Charlie?" He was drifting off to sleep again and her voice startled him.

"Hmmm?" He was barely awake.

She rolled over in his arms.

"Charlie?" Her gentle kiss on his lips woke him up completely.

Her arms went around him, and she snuggled in closer than she'd ever done before, resting her head on his chest. He looked down into her brown eyes and couldn't pull his gaze away.

Her hair fell across the pillow, and he loved to see it there. It reminded him of how lucky he was to have this wonderful woman in his life.

He leaned in and kissed her lightly. But it wasn't enough. His hands cupped her cheeks and he kissed her deeply.

He heard her gasp.

"I, I'm sorry," he said. "I have no right." His guilt overwhelmed him. He had held himself back all this time, but the more time he spent with her, the more he wanted her in every way.

She smiled. "You're my husband. You have every right."

That might be so, but he still felt guilty. "What did you want to tell me, Allie?"

She licked her lips and stared at him. "I don't like sleeping alone in that room. I get scared sometimes."

His heart sank. Did she want to go back home? "Allie," he said softly. "Please don't leave me. I've grown to…. care about you."

She studied his face. "Go back home? Are you crazy?" She looked shocked, terrified even. "I can't go back there. No, I won't be leaving you Charlie Jones." She stared at him, and he wondered what it was she wanted.

"I want to sleep in your bed – with you." She said it quickly, as though she had to get it out hurriedly to make everything alright.

He grinned.

"It's just that, well, I feel safe here with you Charlie."

He sighed. She had him worried there for a minute. "Of course you can sleep with me. Tomorrow we'll move your things in here." He kissed her forehead, and she rolled over to go to sleep.

Charlie pulled her closer. All was right with their little world. Perhaps one day they would become truly married. Maybe she might even come to love him, like he loved her.

He drifted off to sleep with that wonderful thought in his mind.

* * *

Allie strolled down to the butcher shop. She waved to Charlie as she went past the Barber Shop. The shop was empty of customers, and he waved back.

Her heart skipped a beat.

She was becoming more and more fond of her husband, and never wanted to be away from him.

"Good morning Mr Simpson," she said to the butcher. "I'd like some meat for stewing please." Mr Simpson nodded and brought back a quantity he knew to be what Allie always needed.

"Perfect. Thank you. Put it on Charlie's account?" The butcher nodded, and she was on her way again.

Once home, she braised the meat in the pot, then peeled, chopped, and added the vegetables she needed, as well as the stock.

She pulled out the ingredients to make a lemon cake, and as soon as it was cooking, she began to prepare Charlie's lunch. She most often made thick vegetable soup with either biscuits or bread.

Today though, she'd bought fish from Mr Simpson, so would make fish and vegetables. Charlie was sure to enjoy a change.

She took him mid-morning coffee and cake – she'd become accustomed to taking it in each day. At first, she believed it was because Charlie was always hungry and that would appease him, but she came to realize it was more because her heart gave a little skip whenever he was near.

She had become extremely fond of her dear husband, and hoped he felt the same.

By the time the lemon cake was cooked, and she was able to stop by, the shop was full of customers. It was the busiest she'd ever seen it. He barely had time to sweep up the hair before the next customer sat in the barber's chair.

She took the broom from him. "Here, let me Charlie," she said. "You take care of your customers."

His face lit up, and she felt a tingle race from her head to her toes.

As she swept the floor, she gazed at him out of the corner of her eye. He was truly handsome, and she wondered why he hadn't married before.

But of course, she knew the answer – there were way more men in Dayton Falls than women. And the women that were there, were all married.

She was the third mail order bride to arrive and wondered if there would be any more.

"Next!" Charlie's previous customer put some coins in his hand, then grabbed his hat and left.

Allie quickly swept the floor surrounding the chair and moved aside.

After the rush was over and all the customers had left, he took the broom from her, and pulled her close. "Thank you for your help today, Allie," he said, then kissed her forehead. "I don't know what I would have done without your help."

She reveled in his closeness. "That's what I'm here for," she said. "And now I'd better go and make your lunch, or your belly will start to rumble."

She pulled out of his arms, then felt bereft. In his arms is where she felt the happiest.

Chapter Six

Christmas was quickly approaching, and it was time to prepare.

Allie made a list of the items she would need for her Christmas baking. She needed an assortment of raisins, sultanas, currants and prunes, as well as a variety of spices, flour and other necessities.

There were none of the required items in the pantry, so she'd need to go to the Mercantile.

Mr Horvard would be rubbing his hands together when he saw her large list. He might even need to order some items in. But perhaps not, as the other women in town would surely be preparing for their Christmas baking too.

As she entered the store, Mr Horvard's face lit up. Not because it was her per se, she was certain, but because he was certain of another sale.

"Good Morning Mrs Jones. How can I help you on this chilly December day?"

Allie pulled her coat tighter around herself. It seemed quite ridiculous to wear her coat when she was literally crossing the road, but it was always cold in the Mercantile.

"Good day to you too, Mr Horvard," she said. "I have a list of items I need for my Christmas baking."

He grinned. "Ah yes, Christmas. I'm very much behind in putting up my decorations this year." He took her list and looked it over. "I have most of these items, but a few are on order and should arrive in a few days.

"That's fine, thank you very much."

"I'll gather up the items I have in stock and get the Peters boy to bring them over later. They'll be far too heavy for you to carry."

She had no idea what he meant. "The Peters boy?"

He frowned at her. "Young Tommy Peters. He does my deliveries after school. So if you can wait that long, he'll bring them over later today. No charge of course."

"That sounds wonderful, thank you Mr Horvard. In fact, I need some rum, which I presume you don't stock, so I'll wander down to the hotel to purchase some."

Mr Horvard looked worried. "Indeed we don't, Mrs Jones, but I would advise against going to the hotel alone. It is not safe for a lady such as yourself."

Allie laughed at the suggestion. Not safe? It was at the end of the road – only a half a dozen or so shops down the road in fact. "I promise you Mr Horvard, I will be perfectly safe." After all, what could happen in broad daylight?

"Oh, and I almost forgot. Charlie gave me the money to settle our account." She handed over a wad of cash and turned to leave.

"Do wait for a receipt," the store owner said. "That's a lot of money, and I don't want to be accused of stealing."

"Fair enough." Allie waited for the receipt, then headed out the door where she thought about Mr Horvard's warning about the hotel. She shook her head, that couldn't possibly be right.

Besides, most of the patrons were there at night.

She pulled her thick coat around her a little tighter. Mr Horvard was right – it was chilly today. She waved to Mr Simpson, the butcher, as she strolled past.

Mrs Grogan, the doctor's wife was there getting supplies. She waved too.

Next to the butcher shop was Edna's Diner. It was empty but would fill up for supper. Allie drooled over the beautiful gowns in the window of the dress shop next door. She knew they stocked less formal gowns but was certain there would never be a time she would need such a gown.

Allie sighed. These were the sorts of beautiful gowns Charlotte once wore. She wondered if the young mother missed her old life.

Likely not. Especially when her parents tried to force her to marry a nasty old man.

She quickly moved on and gazed at the beautiful shoes and boots in the next window. They were gorgeous.

She lifted her skirts slightly and looked down at her own worn out shoes. They were plain black shoes with a tiny bow. The heel was almost flat – it needed to be for the amount of running around she'd done when she worked for the Montgomery's.

She wondered if these shoes would survive the harsh Christmas weather in Dayton Falls. She guessed they would have to.

Allie turned and stared across the road to the hotel. She remembered Mr Horvard's words and paused. She again shook her head.

He was over reacting. Of course, he was.

She lifted her skirts and made her way over the dirt road. Allie walked up the steps and into the building, where she waited at the counter for the bartender to arrive.

She'd never been in this sort of establishment in her life. Her heart rate kicked up, and she was beginning to wonder if she should have heeded Mr Horvard's advice.

The room as almost empty except for a couple of older gents who sat at a table together, hugging their glasses.

She stared at them for long moments, then pulled her gaze away. They weren't a threat to her. They were simply sitting and talking to each other.

"Can I help you, Miss?"

Allie was startled. She hadn't heard the bartender arrive, and his voice came out of nowhere.

"I, I…" She needed to compose herself. "Do you have a small bottle of rum," she asked. "I only need a bit for my Christmas baking."

"You and all the other ladies in town," the bartended said. "Several of the town's men have collected rum for their women, but you're the first one to come in alone." He scratched his head. "It's really not that safe for a lady, but never you mind, you're here now," he said. "I think I still have a bottle or two. Wait here and I'll check."

He walked into a storage room off to the side, and Allie stood, twisting her handkerchief in her hands, all the while her worry escalated. He was the second one to warn her about coming to this place.

He'd only been gone a few minutes when she felt an unfamiliar arm around her shoulders.

She startled, and tried to shrug it away. "Hello Missus," one of the older gents said. He was visibly drunk, and now he was falling all over her.

"Excuse me, Sir," she said with a shaky voice. "Would you mind not handling me?" She continued to try and shrug out of his grip, but he wasn't having it. Her heartbeat sped up until she felt quite light-headed.

Being polite hadn't worked, so she opted for righteous indignation. "Get yours hands off me," she said between clenched teeth.

Instead of removing his arm, the man spun her around to face him.

"Give us a kiss," he said, making kissing sounds.

His foul breath was revolting, and Allie leaned back, trying to get out of his reach.

Her head was spinning, and she felt sure she was going to faint, but couldn't do that. Not in this place where anything could happen. What a fool she had been to ignore all the warnings.

"Get your damned hands off my wife, Whitey." Charlie bellowed from the doorway. Both his hands were fisted by his side, and his whole body was rigid.

Allie was never so happy to hear her husband's voice. She almost collapsed against the counter "How did you…?" Honestly, she didn't care how he knew she was there. All she cared about right now was that Charlie was there to keep her safe.

He pulled her against him. "Are you alright," he asked gently. She felt comforted in his arms, and her head began to clear.

She nodded, ever grateful for his presence.

"I needed some rum for the Christmas baking," she said quietly.

Charlie looked down at her, his expression one of anger. "Next time tell me. It's not safe to come here, as you've found out."

Why was he so angry with her? "I'm sorry I made you angry, Charlie," she said. "I was certain it would be okay at this time of day."

He pulled her closer. "I'm not angry with *you*," he said. "It's never okay to come here. Too many drunks. Mr Horvard saw you come down here; he was worried." He stared into her eyes. His anger had dissipated. "I'm just relieved you're okay."

"Last bottle." The bartender reached across and handed her the small bottle of rum. "Oh, hello Charlie. Good to see you."

"Thanks Matt, nice to see you too. This is my wife, Allie." He handed over some notes, and turned to leave, his wife close to his side.

"Congratulations," Matt called after them.

Once outside, Charlie said, "Allie, promise me you'll never come here again. I was in a real panic when Mr Horvard came to tell me."

"Why did he do that?" She was annoyed with the store owner.

Charlie sighed. "It's a dangerous place, Allie. He was very worried when he saw you headed up this way. I'm pleased he did – it means he cares. Just like I do."

He leaned in and kissed her gently, and Allie felt a tingle sliver down her spine. "Come on, let's go home."

Allie had real feelings for this man, not only because he protected her, but the little things he did.

She'd felt it from the moment they met.

She'd looked into his face and her heart had melted. She could see herself loving Charlie from the moment she set eyes on him.

Perhaps one day he might feel the same way about her. She inwardly prayed to God that this would be so.

* * *

Charlie held her close as they made their way back to his shop.

He'd locked the door and put a sign up to say he'd be back soon, and now there was a queue of men standing outside waiting.

"I'm sorry, my love," he said. "But those fellows want a hair cut. We need to talk though…"

Allie brushed his apologies aside. "Your customers have to come first," she said. She wasn't upset about it, he could tell. But he wanted to talk it through. Especially since she was still shaking.

As he unlocked the door, she began to follow him. "I'll be right," he whispered, so only she could hear. "You go home and rest."

She shook her head and he knew she wouldn't. She stood aside for the customers to enter, then went straight for the broom.

As each customer had their hair trimmed, and in some cases, a shave as well, Allie cleaned up the mess afterwards. She whisked the shaving mug away and quickly cleaned it out ready for next time, as well as sweeping the floor until it was spotless.

"That's a pretty missus you have there, Charlie." Joseph Spingler winked at him, but instead of taking it as a joke, Charlie was annoyed.

"You keep your eyes and hands off my missus," he said gruffly. If he'd been thinking rationally, he would have realized Joseph was stringing him along, but the events of earlier had him rattled.

Allie didn't look too happy either.

As the last customer left the shop, Allie moved in to snatch up the shaving mug. Charlie reached for her hand at the same time, and the mug landed on the floor, smashing into tiny pieces.

"I'm sorry…" Allie said, tears coming to her eyes. Suddenly she dropped to the floor and began to pick up the pieces, her eyes never leaving him.

"Allie, it's fine," he said. "Nothing to worry about." He lifted his hand to help her up, and she scuttled backwards.

He was confused. What was going on? He put his hands behind his head and grimaced, the whole time staring down at her. Why was his wife acting this way?

As he brought his hands down again, she looked petrified.

"Please don't beat me," she said quietly, tears streaming down her face, her hands protecting it.

Charlie stood rigid. "Beat you? Allie, I…."

She cowered in the corner of the store, under the counter. Charlie turned and locked the door to ensure no customers entered. Then he pulled down the blinds.

She pulled her knees up and wrapped her arms around them, as though she was trying to hide.

It suddenly all made sense.

The bruises. The subservient behavior. She'd been beaten into submission at some point, and not very long ago.

His heart beat quickened, and he could feel his anger boiling over.

But Charlie knew he had to stay calm for Allie. Had to reassure and comfort her, not give in to the fury that surged through him.

He squatted down next to her and pulled her close. Her whole body was stiff. "Allie," he said quietly. "You're safe here. I won't hurt you, I thought you'd know that by now."

"Why," she sniffed. "Why did you close the blinds then?"

He pulled her even closer and rubbed circles over her back. "I did that to ensure no one could see how upset you are. I'm trying to protect you, not hurt you."

As he pulled her to her feet, he pulled her close to his chest. "My darling Allie," he said softly. "What have they done to you?"

He felt her stiffen again. "I wasn't going to tell you," she said. "Because I didn't want you to think badly of me." Her arms crept up around his back, and her head rested on his chest. Tears began to flow again, and he held her tightly.

"No matter what's happened in your past, I want you as my wife." He stroked her hair and held her close to his heart.

Allie sobbed. "I, I was a maid, a servant," she said quickly. "And the Master beat me all the time, for no reason." She looked up at him, tears still welled in those beautiful brown eyes. "I had to leave because I was sure he would kill me one day."

Charlie felt hollow. How could he make things right for his dear wife?

She began to cry again, and he held her like he'd never let her go. And of course, he didn't want to let her go – ever.

Charlie scooped her up in his arms and carried her to the door putting her down only long enough to pull up the blinds and leave the shop.

"Where are we going," she whispered looking into his eyes.

"I'm taking you home. You need to rest."

He carried her around to their home, then laid her on the bed, their bed, where he sat next to her for what seemed like hours. He rubbed circles over her back until she fell asleep, then quietly slipped out and returned to work.

His heart was breaking, but he had to stay strong for Allie – the love of his life.

* * *

When Allie awoke, she was dazed. She knew it wasn't night-time because the room wasn't in darkness. But she couldn't fathom why she was in bed.

Then suddenly she remembered.

Her whole horrible ordeal came crashing back into her memory. She should have told Charlie from the start, then none of this would have happened.

She sighed. It probably would, but at least he would have known the reason why.

She sat rigid on the side of the bed for what seemed an eternity. Then suddenly heard movement in the kitchen.

She gasped.

Oh my gosh, she'd probably slept through Charlie's lunch break. What a horrible, horrible wife he must think her.

She scurried out to the kitchen to find her husband sitting at the table eating a sandwich and drinking coffee.

The moment he saw her he stood. "Are you feeling any better, my love?"

"Much better, thank you," she said, fussing about the room. Had he really said *my love*?

He strolled over to her and pulled out a chair. "You sit. I'm sorted for lunch. I hope it was alright to use the bread."

She stared at him and nodded. "Yes, of course. But I haven't done a thing all day. What a terrible wife I am."

As he placed a mug of tea in front of her, he rubbed circles over her back. "You've had a terrible time of it, Allie." His expression dared her to disagree. "Just sit back and relax. Drink your tea."

"But I haven't prepared anything for supper," she wailed, on the brink of hysteria, remembering all the events of the day.

Charlie saw right through her. "You don't have to slave over a hot stove every day for me." He cupped her face with his hands, and gently kissed her lips. Allie felt a warmth spread through her.

"We could have pancakes for supper tonight," he said, grinning at her. Pancakes were generally reserved for breakfast, but he wanted to be frivolous, so pancakes it was.

She nodded her head, not letting him see how much his kiss had affected her.

"If you want something to do, you could bring all your things into the main bedroom."

She felt the heat creep up her face at the suggestion. They hadn't discussed anything more than actually being in the same bed, but still, Charlie was a man…

She slapped her hands to her cheeks.

"You are so cute when you are embarrassed," he said, pulling her hands away to kiss her cheek. "I have to go back to work. Don't overdo it."

She stood to give him a proper goodbye, and his hands went to her hips. She moved in close and his arms went up around her. "My dear wife," he said. "You really do make it difficult for a man to leave."

He kissed her cheek again. "Unfortunately, I must leave. I'll be back later."

He went to the door and turned to stare back at her before he left. "I miss you already," he said, then quickly closed the door, leaving Allie staring at the shut door.

"Not as much as I'll miss you," she whispered to the empty room.

Chapter Seven

The shop was quiet after lunch, so Charlie decided to close up early and surprise his wife. He had never done that before, and it felt liberating.

Allie was more important to him than anything in the whole world. He hadn't wanted to leave her at lunch time, and had felt incredibly guilty for the next hour, as he sat around waiting for non-existent customers.

"Allie, I'm home," he called as he strolled in the door.

She came running out of the spare room. "Wha…..? What are you doing home?" Her arms were full of clothes as she moved them from one room to the other.

He followed her into the main bedroom and threw the clothes on the bed. They'd barely hit the bed when he scooped her up into his arms. "Oh, how I've missed you," he said, as he pulled her close.

"Silly," she said. "You've hardly been gone anytime."

Instead of answering, he covered her lips with his own. Despite wanting more, it was a chaste kiss. He didn't want to scare her.

Her arms went up around his neck, and Charlie savored her response. "You taste good," he said, then cupped her face and stared into her chocolate brown eyes. "Allie," he said, having his words planned out in his head.

He wanted desperately to say "I love you" but instead pulled her closer.

"I thought we might go for a trip this afternoon," he said quickly. "To pick out a Christmas tree."

She pulled out of his arms, then squealed and jumped with joy. "Oooooooooooooh, really? How exciting!"

He stood planted to the spot, watching his beloved wife dancing around the room. Until she realized he was staring at her.

"Too much?" She shrugged her shoulders. "I've never had a Christmas tree before. Not in my own house, anyway."

"My dear girl, you have certainly missed out." He reached for her coat and helped her into it. "You'll need your gloves as well. It's very cold outside."

The excitement suddenly left Allie's face. "How will we get the tree," she asked. "We don't have a wagon." She looked very deflated.

"Angus and Charlotte are lending us theirs."

It wasn't long until they were on their way, all rugged up in the wagon, sharing a blanket over their knees.

Allie sat close to Charlie, snuggling in to keep warm; he wasn't going to complain. They traveled for about half an hour, until they came to a copse of trees. All they could see were Christmas trees of various sizes. Some big, some small, some narrow, and others wide.

Charlie brought the wagon to a standstill and tied the reins to the branch of one of the trees. He took a saw from the back of the wagon.

"Which one do you want?" He stood staring at her for long moments.

Allie shook her head. "I have no idea," she said. "You choose."

He walked around for a few minutes, then decided. "This one will fit perfectly in our sitting room. Perhaps next to the fire place?"

Allie clapped her hands together excitedly, and he began to cut the tree down with vigor. He'd not bothered before. Why worry when there is no one to share it with?

"Is that," she looked up to the sky excitedly. "Is that snow?"

Charlie stopped what he was doing to check. He grinned. "Just the beginnings. A few flakes here and there. Nothing to get excited about." He went back to cutting the tree.

"It's exciting to me," she said, a little deflated. "I've never seen snow before, Charlie Jones."

He watched as she danced around, catching the snowflakes with her gloved hands. She picked up pieces of fir that had broken off the trees, as well as a handful of small pine cones. To make a decoration, she'd told him.

She was like a child let loose in a sweet shop, but he didn't care.

He was surprised but overjoyed at the same time. It would be like experiencing Christmas for the first time, all through the eyes of his beautiful wife.

* * *

"There, it's ready to be decorated now." Charlie stood up after placing the tree near the fireplace.

Allie couldn't wait to decorate it, then sit back in one of the chairs and stared at it, with her darling husband by her side.

This was their tree. *Their very own tree, cut down with their very own hands.* Well, okay, Charlie's hands.

But it was their first Christmas together, and they would start their own traditions. It was all Allie could do not to cry.

Tomorrow she would go to the Mercantile and buy some red ribbon to decorate the tree.

"Oh, Charlie. It's magnificent." She near flung herself into his arms. Charlie didn't complain.

They stood their holding each other as though the world was about to end, and they were saying their last good-byes. But this was just the beginning, not the end.

"You're such a good man, Charlie Jones," she whispered.

He held her a little tighter, and a thrill shot down her spine. "And you're such a good woman, Allie Jones."

He put his fingers under her chin and turned her face up toward him. Her heart did a little dance when his lips brushed hers. She wondered if his heart was dancing too.

* * *

Charlie walked into the kitchen when Allie was almost ready to cook the pancakes.

He'd been finishing moving her things from the spare room into the main bedroom. Their bedroom. Where they were about to start their *real* married life.

Up until now it had felt like a pretense. Real married couples sleep together. At least that's what Allie had always believed.

Charlotte and Angus slept together. Her parents slept together. Even the Montgomery's slept together. So it must be true, real married couples did sleep in the same bed.

The syrup was on the table, along with butter, and the table settings.

She poured him a coffee and placed it on the table. "You nearly ready for supper?"

He came up behind her and wrapped his arms around her middle, then leaned in and kissed her cheek. "Whenever you're ready," he said. "Are you feeling better tonight?"

She stiffened in his arms. "Yes, thank you," she said uncomfortably. Why did he have to bring the whole horrible incident up again?

"I missed you earlier today," he whispered. "I couldn't stay away any longer."

She leaned back against him, the conversation of minutes ago forgotten already. "I missed you too," she told him. "I always miss you when you're not here."

Allie pulled out of his arms. "I have to make supper. The pan will get too hot and they'll burn. Then what will you eat?"

She turned her head in time to see him grin. "Charlie Jones!" she said briskly. "You go and sit at the table and drink your coffee. Supper will be along shortly."

"You're blushing," he whispered just moments before he went to sit down.

Allie ignored him but knew he was right. She'd felt the heat creep up her face.

She poured the pancake batter into the pan and once cooked, placed the pancakes onto a platter in the middle of the table. Charlie ate while she cooked the second batch.

"Sit down, Allie," he told her. "I like it when you eat with me."

She turned to look at him. He seemed sad. "I'll be there in just a minute. Eat up – there's plenty more coming."

He nodded and reached for more syrup. "These are really good. Where did you learn to cook like this?"

She glared at him.

"Oh. Sorry."

She waved her hands in front of herself. "Sorry. I shouldn't be so sensitive. But I will be forever grateful to Cook. When she needed help, I was always her first choice." She leaned over as she added the remaining pancakes to the platter.

Charlie pulled her into his lap, and her heart fluttered. "I'm glad you were too. You're an amazing cook."

She felt heat rise up her face – again. "Thanks Charlie."

"Now go and eat while they're still hot." He reached over and piled a few of the freshly cooked items onto her plate.

"Tomorrow we'll have something special," she said, taking her seat. "Don't ask me what, because I don't know yet."

Charlie laughed as he tucked into one of his most favorite foods.

* * *

After supper they finished moving her clothes into the main room, then proceeded to add them to the wardrobe.

They'd had to shuffle Charlie's things around, but he didn't mind. It was nice to finally have his wife in his room.

It must have been difficult for her, marrying a stranger within minutes of them meeting. It was difficult for him too, but at least he was in familiar territory. Allie was in a strange place, with a strange man.

He wondered who she would have married if it hadn't been him, and who he might have married. He shook the thought away.

He had Allie now, and that was all that mattered.

Not that there were single women in town, because there weren't. It was the reason he'd reached out to a mail order bride agency. And he was so glad he did.

He could hear Allie clattering around in the kitchen, finishing up the dishes and putting them away.

He lit the fire in the bedroom while he waited for her. The nights were quite cold now, and the room was chilly. Allie had hated the spare room she'd told him, but had said she was frightened. He hadn't thought to light a fire in there for her. That might have helped?

He began to undress once the fire was going; he removed his shoes and belt, and began to undo the buttons of his shirt, pulling it out of his pants.

He brushed his hair back off his face.

Charlie stood as his wife entered the room. "Allie," he said. "I'm sorry, I meant to be changed into my nightshirt before you got in here."

She stared at him. Had she never seen a man half undressed before? Probably not, he realized.

He studied her as she slowly moved towards him.

She gaped at his hair-covered chest and wrapped her arms around him.

She stood on her tippy toes and lightly kissed his lips, then slunk down again. "You're very beautiful, Charlie Jones," she told him softly.

He loved when she used his full name. It was an endearment he'd come to love.

His hands went up to her face, and he stared into her coppery eyes. His heart began to race, and he knew he'd always be with this woman. His wife.

The love of his life.

"You are beyond beautiful," he told her quietly. He leaned in and kissed her neck.

With shaking hands, he began to undo the buttons down the front of her dress. He couldn't wait to consummate this marriage – he was so in love with his wife.

But he vowed to be gentle with her.

He watched as her dress slid to the floor and exposed her full beauty. He pulled his shirt off, as he laid her gently on the bed. "Allie, my love," he said quietly, pulling the covers up over her. The last thing he wanted was for her to be cold.

"I know I've never said it before," he said with a voice he didn't recognize. It was not his voice; this voice was too husky with anticipation. "But I have fallen in love with you, my sweet Allie. I love you with all my heart." He was light-headed with happiness to have finally told her how he felt.

She looked surprised. "Oh Charlie," she said with a smile on her face. "I've loved you almost from the start. You make me feel things I have no right to feel."

He was grinning, he knew he was, but he didn't care. His Allie loved him. And he loved her.

His life couldn't get any better than it was right now.

Chapter Eight

Allie woke with Charlie's arms wrapped around her, as she often did after she'd climbed into his bed in the night.

But today was different. Today she was a woman. A proper married woman who was intensely in love with her husband.

She slid out of bed, leaving Charlie to sleep, but his arm snaked around her waist and pulled her back. He leaned up over her and looked down into her face. "Good morning my love," he said softly.

She smiled up at him. "Good morning, husband," she said quietly. "I slept much better last night, because I was in your bed."

He winked at her. "It wasn't because you were in here. And it's *our* bed now."

She felt the heat creep quickly up her face. She wished she could control her embarrassment.

He leaned into her and gently brushed her lips.

"Charlie," she scolded. "I have to get up. I have things to do."

She pulled away and slid out of the warm bed, made warmer by the fact her husband was in it. She drew her soft robe up around herself and patted into the kitchen, ready to light the fire for Charlie's coffee.

"I can do that. You sit down and rest."

She gazed at him. "I can do it just as easily. You need to get ready for work."

He shrugged his shoulders but lit the fire anyway. When that was done, he lit the sitting room fire too. "It's getting colder now. The closer we get to Christmas, the worse it gets. I don't want you getting sick." He hugged her close, and Allie reveled in his nearness.

"I hope Mr Horvard has plenty of red ribbon in stock," she said, trying to change the subject. She knew how distracted Charlie could get when he got all lovey-dovey on her.

She pulled out of his arms and moved to the kitchen. She stared out the window, glued to the spot. "Charlie, Charlie," she called urgently, and he came running.

He had terror written all over his face. "What's wrong, what's happened," he demanded, as he entered the room.

Allie laughed, and pointed out the window. "Look! It's snowing. Real snow this time, not just a few flakes like when we got the Christmas tree!" She headed to the door. "I want to go out and play in it. I've never touched snow before."

She felt Charlie's hand cover hers as she tried to open the door. "You need to get dressed first, and rug up, including gloves. Otherwise you'll end up with frost-bite."

He reached around with his free hand and pulled her against him. "I'm going to miss you today," he whispered. "More than ever." He spun her around in his arms and kissed her forehead.

She glanced up at him from under her lashes. "First, you have to go to work. Otherwise there's nothing to miss. You get ready while I make your breakfast," she said sternly.

He laughed a big belly laugh, and it warmed Allie from her head to her toes. She'd never heard him laugh like that before.

"Shoo," she told him, motioning with her hands. "By the time you are dressed, your omelet will be ready."

He scurried off into the bedroom to change as Allie worked in the kitchen.

She turned to watch him go and wondered how she'd been so lucky as to get a man like him.

* * *

Sunday came around quickly.

Allie donned her Sunday best dress, and Charlie stood back and admired her. "You look beautiful, Mrs Jones," he said. He enjoyed watching her blush, but every word he said was true.

The church was a short walk away, but he helped Allie into her warm coat, and made sure she put on her gloves.

He knew she looked forward to church, because she got to catch up with Charlotte, as well as some of the other ladies from church.

It must get lonely for her during the week. He, on the other hand had plenty of people to talk to in the way of customers.

He'd watched her when she helped in the barber shop and the customers conversed with her. Allie's face lit up – she hung on every word they said.

She needed someone to spend her time with, but he wasn't sure who that could be. As much as she and Charlotte were friends, Charlotte had her hands full with her brood of children.

Perhaps one day Allie would have her hands full too. He could only hope.

He carried the hot stew wrapped up in a kitchen towel, ready to share for luncheon at church. It was a highlight of the week for his wife, and in some ways for him too. He took delight in her happiness.

They made their way into a pew at the very back of the church. Allie felt awkward being up the front, she'd told him. The last thing he wanted to do was make her feel out of place. Especially now that she'd finally settled in.

They'd not long taken their places when the music began. *Onward Christian Soldiers* was a favorite for Charlie, and Allie had said it was one of her favorites too. As they stood to begin singing, he put his arm around her shoulders. He said a silent pray and thanked God for sending this angel to him.

What he'd done to deserve her, he'd never know, but he appreciated every moment he got to spend with her.

When the service was over, they moved to the hall where the luncheon would be held. It was just as easy to go home since they lived so close, but Allie enjoyed it so much, he didn't want to let her down.

The Ladies Auxiliary women rallied around and organised the food, while the men sat talking. Several of the town's men congratulated him on his recent marriage.

The pastor came over and sat beside him. "How are things going with your young bride, Charlie?" He'd made it known some time again he was not an advocate of mail order bride marriages. *Marriage should be based on love*, he'd told Charlie.

But Charlie knew love could grow over time. It certainly had for him.

He fiddled with his hat on his lap. "It's going really well, Pastor," he said. "We are very much in love."

The pastor patted him on the back. "Good to hear, young fella." Then he stood and walked away to chat with another parishioner.

Allie appeared from the kitchen, her hands laden with food. He jumped up to help her, but she clearly didn't need his help. She was in her element, helping out, while at the same time getting to meet other women, and hopefully make new friends.

Angus came to sit beside him. "She's fine, my friend," he said. "Leave her to get to know everyone."

Charlie nodded. Angus had been through the exact same thing, and not all that long ago. "You two getting on alright?"

He stared at the sheriff and grinned.

Angus slapped him on the back. "Charlotte will be happy. She's been anxious, worrying about the two of you, but especially Allie."

Charlie leaned in so only Angus could hear. "Tell her not to worry. We're doing fine."

* * *

Allie was pleased to discover the Mercantile had plenty of red ribbon, and she spent much of the morning creating bows to hang on the Christmas tree.

She stood back and stared at her handiwork – it looked beyond beautiful, especially with the fire burning beside it.

She was certain Charlie would be pleased.

She spent the rest of the morning preparing a roast for dinner, baking bread, and organizing Charlie's lunch – sausages and fried potatoes.

This afternoon she would get to work on the decoration. She had planned to use the sprigs she'd collected from the forest, as well as the small pine cones she'd found.

The door opened as she was pouring Charlie's coffee. She was excited to show him the tree and greeted him warmly with a hug.

"I could take this every day when I come home for lunch," he said, a smile on his face.

Allie looked up at him expectantly. "I have a surprise," she said, dragging him into the sitting room and pushing him down into a chair. "I can only imagine sitting down here at night and watching it for hours."

Charlie stared at it. "You did an amazing job," he said. "But I'm not sure I want to watch it for hours. I have better things to do with my time." He wiggled his eyebrows at her.

Allie stood with her hands on her hips. "Charlie Jones, you are incorrigible."

She returned to the kitchen and dished up his lunch.

As he sat eating with obvious enjoyment, Allie picked at her food.

"Is there a problem," Charlie asked. "You seem to be playing with your food." He studied her keenly.

Her head shot up. "Not a problem exactly…." She put her knife and fork down on her plate. "I've been trying to plan for Christmas supper. Will it just be the two of us? What do you normally do for Christmas?"

She studied him; he looked uncomfortable. "Charlie?" He continued to eat, totally ignoring her question. That wasn't like him at all.

He looked up momentarily and answered. "I've never done anything special. Sandwich for lunch, cold or cooked beans for supper."

That made her incredibly sad. Her own family, as poor as they were, still celebrated the Lord's birth in the best way they could, and with family surrounding them.

"But… what about your family? Your mother….?"

He pushed his hair back from his face. "Both dead," he said with emotion. "A wagon accident some years ago. The horses were killed as well."

"Oh Charlie!" She ran to his side and hugged him tight, but he shrugged her away.

"Let it be, woman," he snapped, pushing her away.

Allie had never seen him like this. "I'm sorry if I upset you," she said. "But I care about you."

He gazed into her eyes. "I know," he said quietly. "But I don't like to talk about it."

Suddenly he jumped to his feet. "I have to get back to work," he said hurriedly.

Allie hugged him extra tight as he was leaving. "Allie, I…" He stared down into her eyes and brushed the hair back from her face. "Don't be sad. I'm sorry I acted like an ass."

She continued to stare at him. "You have every right," she said. "Losing family is hard. I can't imagine what you went through."

She pushed up on her toes and kissed him gently. "Would you like me to come and help this afternoon?" Perhaps her presence would cheer him up.

"I'll be fine. You do whatever you had planned."

He gave her an extra squeeze and was on his way.

Allie stood staring after him for an eternity. This Christmas was going to be special. This was going to be a Christmas that Charlie would remember for a very long time.

She would make sure of it.

Chapter Nine

Allie spent the afternoon on her Christmas baking.

She made cookies, muffins, and mince pies. With a little under a week to go, she had to get more organized – with everything.

She'd bought some wool from the Mercantile about a week back and had begun to knit a scarf for Charlie as a Christmas gift. She didn't know what else to get him, but had noticed he didn't have a scarf, so it seemed perfect.

She hoped he liked it.

She iced the muffins and once cool, added little sprigs of holly as decoration. She didn't ice the cookies, but left them bare, adding them to an airtight tin to keep fresh.

Tomorrow she would bake a Christmas cake, as well as a pudding. Charlie wouldn't know what hit him – this Christmas would be his best ever.

At least she hoped it would be.

She stood in the doorway to the sitting room staring at the tree. How beautiful it was, but she felt something was still missing.

She pondered for a few minutes, then realized it was candles. It needed to be lit up, and would look so beautiful at night, with the fire roaring beside it.

She'd seen some in the pantry, so ran to check it out.

She found ten hidden in a box in the corner. Not quite as many as she'd hoped, but she would make do.

Allie secured them on some of the branches, ready to light tonight when Charlie was home. It would be *their* tradition – lighting the candles together.

She returned to the kitchen and began work on her decorations. She'd found some thin wire, which she used to put the branches together. She formed them into a circle along with a few of the pine cones.

Then she added a big red ribbon to the center.

She smiled at the result.

Allie added it to the front door, then stood back and admired her handiwork. It was truly beautiful.

Snowed flittered down onto her nose, and she brushed it away. It hit her head and she shook her head to get rid of it.

She looked up to the sky – the snow was beautiful. Sure, it was cold when it hit her skin, but it was such a beautiful sight for someone who had never seen snow before.

Perhaps she could convince Charlie to make a snowman later?

She went back inside; she was starting to get cold. She still had a lot of twigs and pine cones left, so decided to make a similar decoration for Charlie's Barber Shop.

She put her finger to her chin – where would it go?

If he didn't want to hang it on the door, it could go on the mirror. She hurried to make the second Christmas wreath. This one was just as beautiful as the first. There were still some items left over, so she hung them around the house, making it look even more festive.

She'd been so engrossed in what she was doing, Allie hadn't realized how late it was – until she heard the door open.

She ran to her husband and hugged him tight. "Oh Charlie," she said. "I've had such a lovely day making decorations."

He held the door open and stared at the decoration there. "So I see," he said. "But it's not very secure. Let me fix it – I'd hate for it to fall down."

Her face fell. Didn't he like it? "It's very beautiful," he finally said. Was it her expression that coaxed him into saying so?

"Do you really like it, Charlie?" she asked.

He nodded as he hammered a small nail into the door. "That's better. It won't fall now." He snaked his arm around her and pulled her close. "I adore it," he said. "I've never seen anything like it."

She was feeling a little insecure, but Allie had no idea why. "You might think I'm some silly little girl," she said. "But I made one for your shop as well. You don't have to use it if you don't want to."

She reluctantly pulled herself away from him, lifted it from the kitchen counter to show him.

Charlie's eyes opened wide. "Another beauty!" he said. "You're very talented, wife of mine," he said affectionately.

"Oh!" she said suddenly. "I've got another surprise for you." She led him into the sitting room.

He stared at her handiwork once more. "The tree will look stunning in the night light with the candles lit," he said, pulling her close.

Warmth spread through Allie, and an excited thrill raced down her spine.

She knew she was exactly where she needed to be. Her life had changed tremendously over the past weeks, but she was so happy.

All she wanted now was to give Charlie the best Christmas he'd ever had.

Chapter Ten

Allie's eyes blinked open. It was Christmas Day!

Charlie was still asleep, which was exactly what she wanted. She pulled her robe up around herself and snuck out of the bedroom.

She lit the oven, then the sitting room fire. It was colder today than it had been for weeks. Charlie had warned her, but she thought he'd been exaggerating.

She added water to the kettle before putting it on the stove, then stared out the window.

It was snowing.

Not just a light splattering, but heavily. It looked magical. She resisted the urge to run outside and play in it.

She prepared the turkey for lunch, and once the oven was hot enough, she would put it in there as it would take quite some time to cook.

She'd cleaned the whole house from top to bottom over the past few days, made a table decoration, which she'd hidden from her husband as a last-minute surprise, and had the Christmas pudding ready to be boiled later today.

She took a deep breath.

What else did she need to do? She'd forgotten something, she was certain of it.

She prepared Charlie's mug with coffee, ready for when he got up, and made herself a cup of tea. She set the table for breakfast.

It still niggled away in her mind that something had been forgotten.

Allie sat down at the table and sipped her tea.

She looked up as Charlie plodded out in just his nightgown.

She couldn't help but stare at him. He was so beautiful, this husband of hers.

"Charlie Jones," she said. "It's freezing cold. Get some clothes on yourself!"

Suddenly it hit her. She'd finished Charlie's Christmas gift, but had forgotten to wrap his scarf up. She'd have to find a way to do it without him knowing.

He walked over to her. "Does it bother you to see me like this?" He took her hands and pulled her to him, then wrapped his arms around her. "I'm so glad we met, Allie. I can't imagine my life without you."

She rested her head against his chest.

"I was so lonely before you arrived," he continued. "Lonely and grumpy." He laughed. "And starving half the time. I got very sick of beans."

She looked up into his handsome face. "I'm so sorry you went through that," she told him. "I guess we both had our demons." She lifted her hand to his chin. "You need a shave," she said laughing.

He pulled her a little closer, and Allie thanked the Lord for the day she met Charlie Jones.

He kissed her lightly, then pushed away. "We have a busy day," he said. "There's a short service at the church, and then the rest of the day is ours."

She made his coffee and they drank together before having breakfast, then preparing for church.

* * *

"Happy Christmas," Allie told Charlotte as she hugged her tight outside the Dayton Falls church. Angus held tight to the children, as the women greeted each other.

The two of them held onto each other for what seemed forever. If it wasn't for Charlotte, Allie wouldn't have come here. She might have chosen one of the other men Miss Bethany had to offer. She didn't want to think about it.

She moved to Angus's side. "Merry Christmas, Angus," she said, hugging him.

The music began, and they moved inside.

The service was short, as Charlie had said it would be, and they were lined up to shake the Pastor's hand before they knew it.

They walked hand-in-hand through the snow, back to their humble cottage. "I'm sorry, Charlie," Allie said. "But I'm going to have to replace these worn out shoes." She pulled a face. "My feet are wet from the snow."

Charlie scooped her up and carried her the rest of the short distance home. "Well we certainly can't have that," he said laughing.

When they were inside, he pulled her soaking wet shoes off her feet and got a towel to dry them. Then he presented her with a brightly wrapped gift.

"These are for you, my love," he said. "I think you'll like them."

Her eyes opened wide. "For me? Oh Charlie. You really shouldn't have." She hurried to rip the paper off the gift.

Tears welled up in her eyes, and she flung her arms around his neck. "Oh Charlie," he said. "How did you know? They're beautiful, thank you."

Charlie wiped a tear from her face. "I have my spies," he told her. "Someone told me you'd been eyeing these boots off in the store window." He kneeled down and tried them on her feet. They fitted perfectly.

"I have a gift for you too, Charlie," she said softly. "But it's nothing as elaborate as these." She scurried into the pantry where she'd hidden it and produced another wrapped package.

"You didn't have to…" he began.

Allie held her breath. "It's not much," she said. "But I knew it was something you could use."

He pulled the hand knitted scarf out of the package and wrapped it around his neck. "It's perfect and will certainly keep me warm. Thank you, my love."

He pulled her into his lap, and they held each other for long minutes.

"I have to get lunch organized," she told him, then pulled away.

The turkey was already in the oven, and Allie added the vegetables. She took the white tablecloth from the linen press and added it to the table, then set it with the best of their crockery and cutlery, and added red linen napkins she'd managed to get on sale at the Mercantile last month.

Then she added the centerpiece she'd made.

"That looks magnificent," Charlie said, entering the room. "You've gone to way too much trouble." He leaned in and kissed her forehead.

"Nothing is too much trouble for you, Charlie Jones," she said, her voice full of emotion.

She checked the oven, then turned back to him. "Lunch is nearly ready, so don't go taking off anywhere."

Charlie took a bottle of wine from the pantry and placed it in the middle of the table. Allie stared at him. "I've been saving it for a special occasion," he said. "Besides, I couldn't drink a whole bottle on my own." He poured a small amount into each glass and sat down when Allie instructed him to do so.

She was about to dish up their Christmas lunch, when there was a soft tap at the door.

"Who the heck would that be," Charlie asked her, confusion on his face.

She was as confused as he was. "No idea."

They opened the door to find a group of carolers standing there. He pulled his wife close and stood glued to the spot as they were entertained with Christmas songs.

Allie was close to tears. She'd promised to make her husband's Christmas special, and this had been the icing on the cake.

Epilogue

Five months later…

"Charlie, Charlie. Come quick!"

He ran from the bedroom quicker than he'd ever done before. "What's wrong?" He was out of breath and near panting.

"Quick, give me your hand." Allie snatched his hand up and placed it on her belly.

He stood there gawking. Her belly was moving. Really moving.

"What the heck is this?" he said, dumbfounded. He shook his head in disbelief. "Should I call for Doc Grogan? Perhaps you should lay down."

He scooped her up in his arms and headed for the bedroom. "You lay here. I'll be back shortly with the doc."

"Charlie," she said softly. But he wasn't listening. "Charlie!" she said more forcefully.

He stuck his head around the door. "I have to get the doc. I'll be back soon. You just rest up."

"Charlie," she said softly again. "Come over here." She patted a spot on the bed next to her.

He did as he was told but was still worried.

"Give me your hand, Charlie," she whispered. His hand stiffened. "Relax," she said laughing.

He was confused. Why was she laughing.

"Charlie Jones," she said softly. "Let me introduce you to your baby – who is currently kicking madly."

Charlie's eyes filled with tears. He thought his wife was dying, but instead, he was going to be a father.

All was right with his world.

From the Author

Thank you so much for reading my book – I hope you enjoyed it.

I would greatly appreciate you leaving a review where you purchased, even if it is only a one-liner. It helps to have my books more visible!

The next book in this series is *The Mercantile Owner's Bride*

About the Author

Multi-published, award-winning and bestselling author Cheryl Wright, former secretary, debt collector, account manager, writing coach, and shopping tour hostess, loves reading.

She writes both historical and contemporary western romance, as well as romantic suspense.

She lives in Melbourne, Australia, and is married with two adult children and has six grandchildren. When she's not writing, she can be found in her craft room making greeting cards.

Links

Website: *http://www.cheryl-wright.com/*

Facebook Reader Group:
https://www.facebook.com/groups/cherylwrightaut hor/

Join My Newsletter:

*https://cheryl-wright.com/newsletter/
(and receive a free book)*